Studio Fun International
An imprint of Printers Row Publishing Group
A division of Readerlink Distribution Services, LLC
10350 Barnes Canyon Road, Suite 100, San Diego, CA 92121
www.studiofun.com

Printers Row Publishing Group is a division of Readerlink Distribution Services, LLC.
Studio Fun International is a registered trademark of Readerlink Distribution Services, LLC.

All notations of errors or omissions should be addressed to Studio Fun International, Editorial Department, at the above address.

ISBN: 978-0-7944-4352-8
Manufactured, printed, and assembled in Shenzhen, China.
First printing, November 2018. RRD/11/18
22 21 20 19 18   1 2 3 4 5

Disney

DUMBO

Early one morning, before the stars had left the sky, a flock of storks flew high over the sleeping countryside, carrying some very special bundles. Inside the bundles were new little baby animals, waiting to be delivered to their mothers.

Far below, the lead stork saw the tents and trailers of a circus. "Release your bundles!" he shouted.

From her pen, Mrs. Jumbo watched the bundles floating down. Surely one of them held her own little baby, she thought, as one parcel after another dropped gently to the ground.

One bundle held a fuzzy little bear cub. A funny baby kangaroo peeked out of another. And in another was a long-necked baby giraffe.

But no special bundle came for Mrs. Jumbo.

As the animals boarded the train the next morning, Mrs. Jumbo did not want to leave. As she climbed into the elephant car, she searched the sky again. Where, oh where was the bundle with her little baby?

"All aboard!" shouted the Ringmaster. "All aboard!"

Casey Junior whistled. With a powerful tug, he headed down the track. Once again the circus was on its way.

Mr. Stork flew down to the little train and landed on the roof of a train car. "Oh, Mrs. Jumbo! Special delivery for Mrs. Jumbo!" he called, hopping from one train car to the next.

From one car, Mr. Stork saw several elephant trunks waving at him. "Yoo-hoo! Yoo-hoo! In here! In here!" the elephants called.

Mr. Stork hopped into the train car. "Which one of you ladies is expecting a little bundle of joy?" he asked.

"Right over there," the elephants answered, pointing to Mrs. Jumbo.

She smiled shyly as Mr. Stork placed the bundle at her feet, cleared his throat, and began to recite, "Here is a baby with eyes of blue, straight from heaven—right to you!"

"Do hurry, dearie," the other elephants urged as Mrs. Jumbo began to untie the bundle with her trunk.

"Oooh!" Everyone cooed when the bundle fell open. For there sat an adorable baby elephant, with a sweet little trunk and big, blue eyes.

"What are you going to call him?" the elephants asked Mrs. Jumbo.

"Jumbo Junior," she replied proudly.

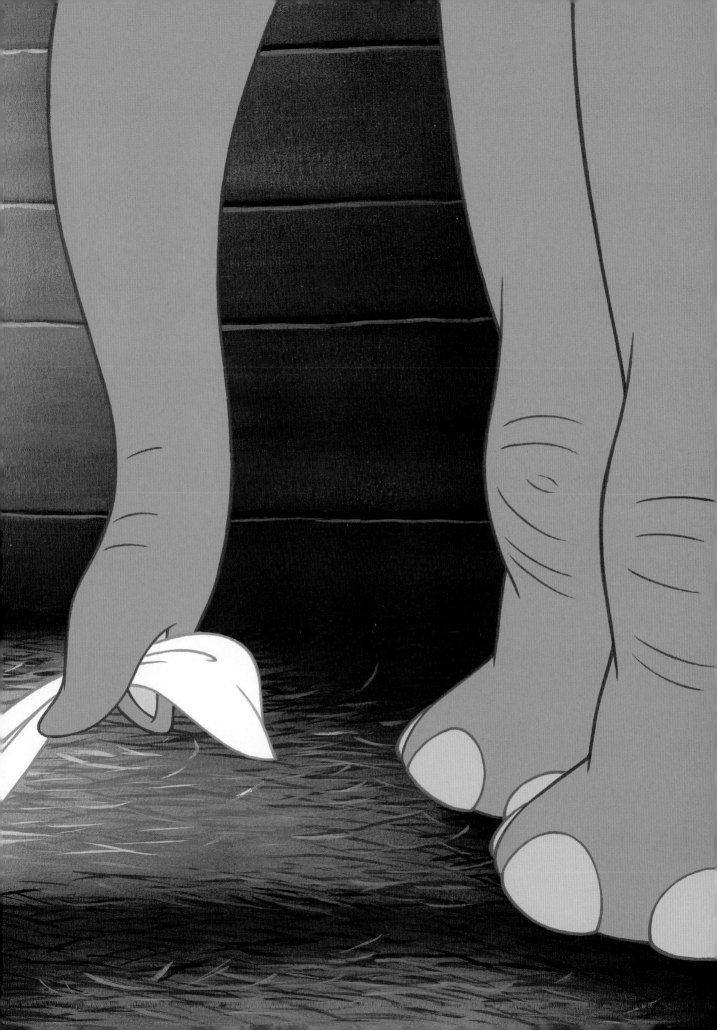

"Kootchy, kootchy, koo!" one elephant said, tickling the baby beneath his chin.

"Aaachoo!" the little elephant sneezed. His ears, which had been neatly tucked behind his head, flopped open. They were enormous!

The elephants shrieked with laughter. "Just look at those ears," one elephant giggled. "Why, with those ears, you should call him 'Dumbo'!"

The elephants' teasing made Mrs. Jumbo angry. Turning her
back on the others, she picked up her baby, carried him to a
corner of the train car, and lay down beside him.

She didn't care if her baby's ears were big. She thought he
was beautiful just the way he was. Cuddling him in her trunk,
she gently rocked him to sleep.

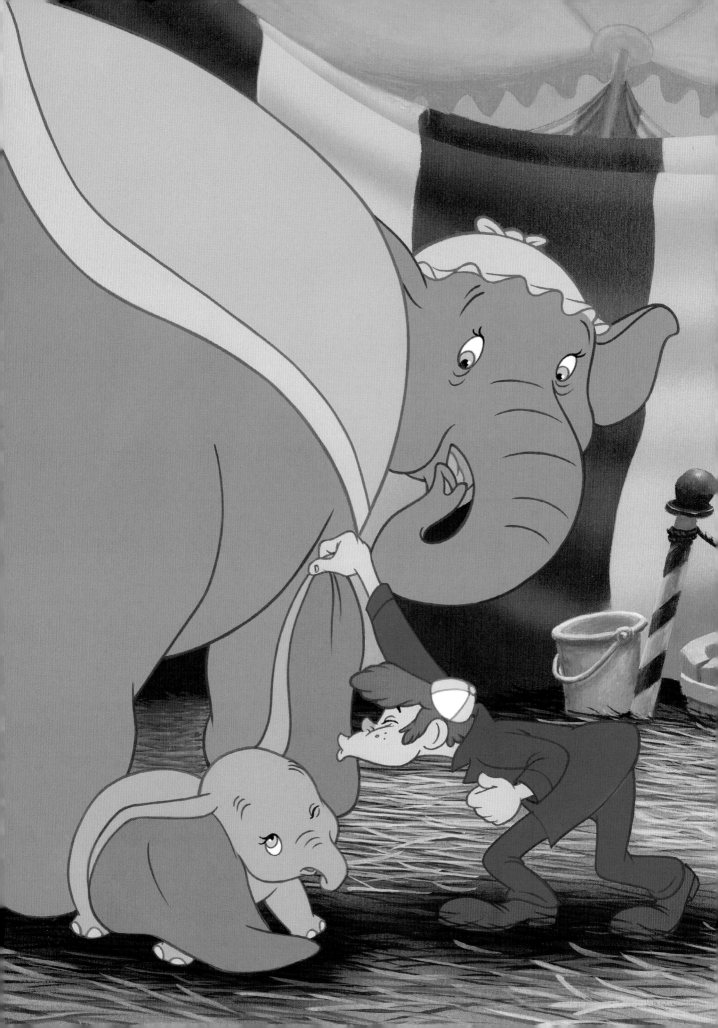

The next day, the townspeople followed the parade to the circus grounds. "Hurry, hurry, hurry! Step right up and get your tickets!" the circus barker called to the gathering crowd.

Inside the elephant tent, Mrs. Jumbo was quietly bathing Dumbo when a bunch of rowdy boys ran in.

"Look at those ears!" they shouted when they saw Dumbo. "Isn't that the funniest thing you ever saw?" The boys wiggled their ears and stuck out their tongues at Dumbo.

Dumbo tried to hide behind his mother,
but the boys wouldn't leave him alone.
Laughing and jeering, they crawled beneath
the ropes and pulled his ears.

Mrs. Jumbo wanted to protect her baby.
She picked up a bale of straw and threw it
at the boys to scare them away.

The Ringmaster dashed into the tent. "Down, Mrs. Jumbo!" he shouted.
Then someone tried to pull Dumbo away. Furious, Mrs. Jumbo bellowed and charged.
"Wild elephant! Wild elephant!" the people screamed, running in all directions.
Animal trainers threw ropes around Mrs. Jumbo, who fought and strained against them.

But Mrs. Jumbo was no match for the men and their strong ropes. At last, she was too exhausted to fight anymore.

"Lock her up," the Ringmaster commanded.

As Dumbo watched, the trainers dragged his mother away. They locked her in a wagon that was set apart from the rest of the circus.

Dumbo's mother was worried about her little one. All she wanted was to cradle him close to her again.

Dumbo, crying for his mother, thought he had no friends in the world as the other elephants turned their backs on him.

But Dumbo was wrong. Someone did want to be his friend. In a corner of the tent sat a little mouse named Timothy. When he saw how the other elephants treated poor Dumbo, it made him mad.

"Look at that poor little fella," the little mouse said. "Everyone's making fun of his ears. What's the matter with them? I think they're cute."

But Dumbo was scared of Timothy, at first. Timothy found him hiding beneath a pile of hay.

"Aw, you aren't afraid of little old me, are you?" Timothy asked. "I'm Timothy Mouse, and I'm your friend, Dumbo.

At that, Dumbo forgot all about being scared. He crawled out of the hay and listened wide-eyed to everything his new friend had to say.

"I know you're embarrassed by your ears, kid," Timothy said. "But lots of people with big ears are famous. So all we gotta do is make you a big star. But first we need a really colossal act. And I'm just the fellow to think of one. Leave everything to me."

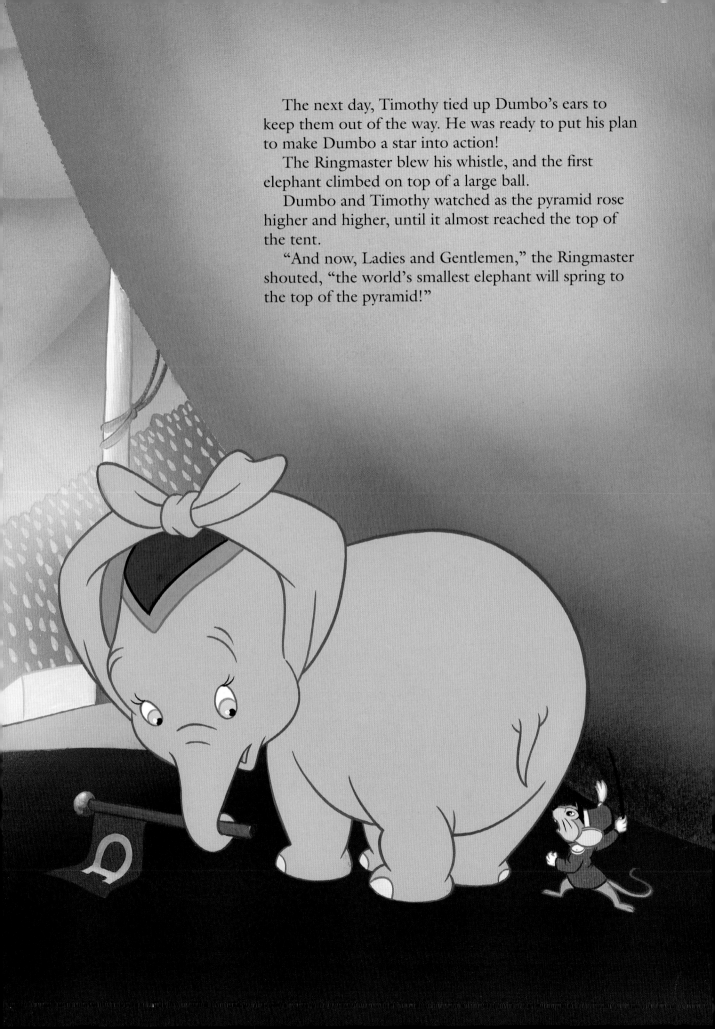

The next day, Timothy tied up Dumbo's ears to keep them out of the way. He was ready to put his plan to make Dumbo a star into action!

The Ringmaster blew his whistle, and the first elephant climbed on top of a large ball.

Dumbo and Timothy watched as the pyramid rose higher and higher, until it almost reached the top of the tent.

"And now, Ladies and Gentlemen," the Ringmaster shouted, "the world's smallest elephant will spring to the top of the pyramid!"

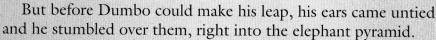

But before Dumbo could make his leap, his ears came untied and he stumbled over them, right into the elephant pyramid.

For a moment, the stunned crowd watched in silence as the elephant pyramid teetered and swayed. Then they ran for their lives as the elephants began to fall.

Trumpeting and bellowing, the elephants tumbled down, crashing into beams and platforms and bleachers. They smacked into walls and pulled down wires and ropes. Finally, they crashed into the center tent pole.

The enormous tent began to sway and billow. Then, with a huge groan, it collapsed and the audience fled to safety. This was an evening at the circus that no one would ever forget!

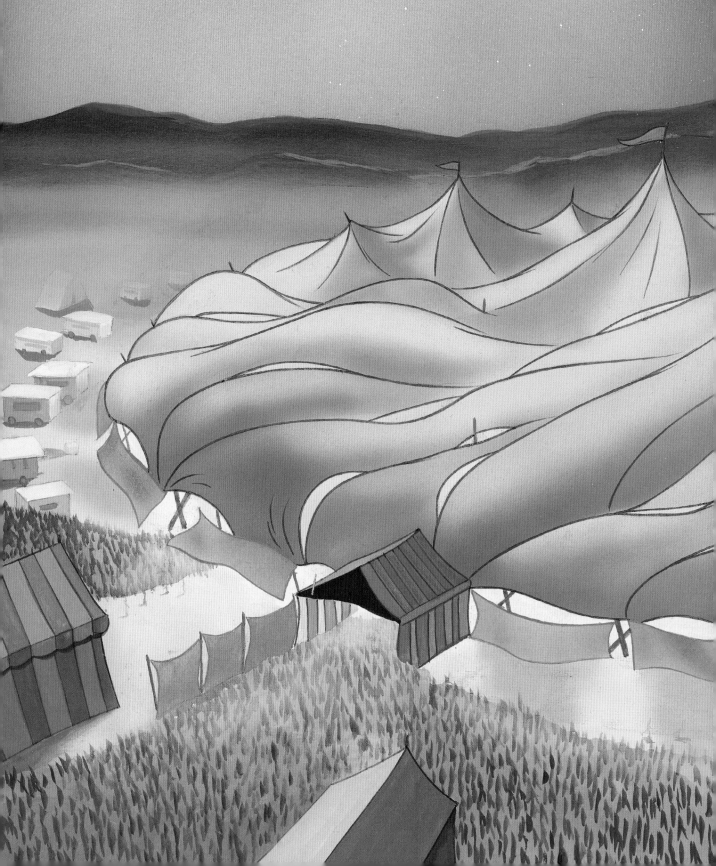

The elephants blamed Dumbo for all that had happened, so he started working with the circus clowns.

The very next show, the clowns painted Dumbo's face and dressed him as a baby. They put him on a tiny platform high up in a building surrounded by crackling, make-believe flames.

Dumbo stood shaking with fear, while far below, clowns dressed as firefighters ran around squirting hoses at each other.

The clown firemen kept throwing water at the burning building, but most of it landed in poor Dumbo's face.

"The baby will have to jump!" the clown fire chief announced. The firefighters held up a thin safety net. Closing his eyes, Dumbo leaped from the building.

Dumbo fell through the net and landed in a tub of wet plaster. The audience roared with laughter. As the clowns bowed to the cheering crowds, they paid no attention to Dumbo, who crept from the tent feeling hurt, humiliated, and miserable.

After the show, the clowns celebrated in their tent.

"Cheer up, Dumbo," Timothy said as he scrubbed his friend's sad little face. "I've found out where they're keeping your mother. I'm going to take you to see her later tonight."

A wistful smile crossed Dumbo's face. Things wouldn't seem so bad if he could just see his mother.

Later that night, while most of the circus folk slept, Timothy took Dumbo to the wagon where his mother was chained.

"Mrs. Jumbo, someone to see you!" Timothy called.

Mrs. Jumbo put her trunk through the bars of the window and stroked Dumbo's head. She wrapped her trunk around Dumbo and rocked him lovingly.

Dumbo cried a little after seeing his mother. All he wanted was to be with her. Once he lay down to sleep, he began to have the strangest dream. In the dream, he was blowing bubbles. Soon, the bubbles looked just like elephants—elephants that danced and flew!

The next morning, Timothy tried to convince
Dumbo that he could fly just like a bird. He said
Dumbo's ears were so big, they were like wings.
Dumbo wasn't so sure, but he trusted Timothy.

In the next show, Dumbo performed
once again with the clowns. They wanted
him to leap from the burning building
again. But this time, Timothy had given a
bird feather to Dumbo. Timothy said it was
a magic feather that would help him fly.

Dumbo felt scared—he was sure the
building was taller this time. But he trusted
Timothy, and so, holding the feather tight,
Dumbo got ready to jump.

It worked! Dumbo and Timothy soared through
the air. But halfway to the bottom, Dumbo lost his
grip on the magic feather. Without it, he couldn't fly.
He and Timothy were falling!

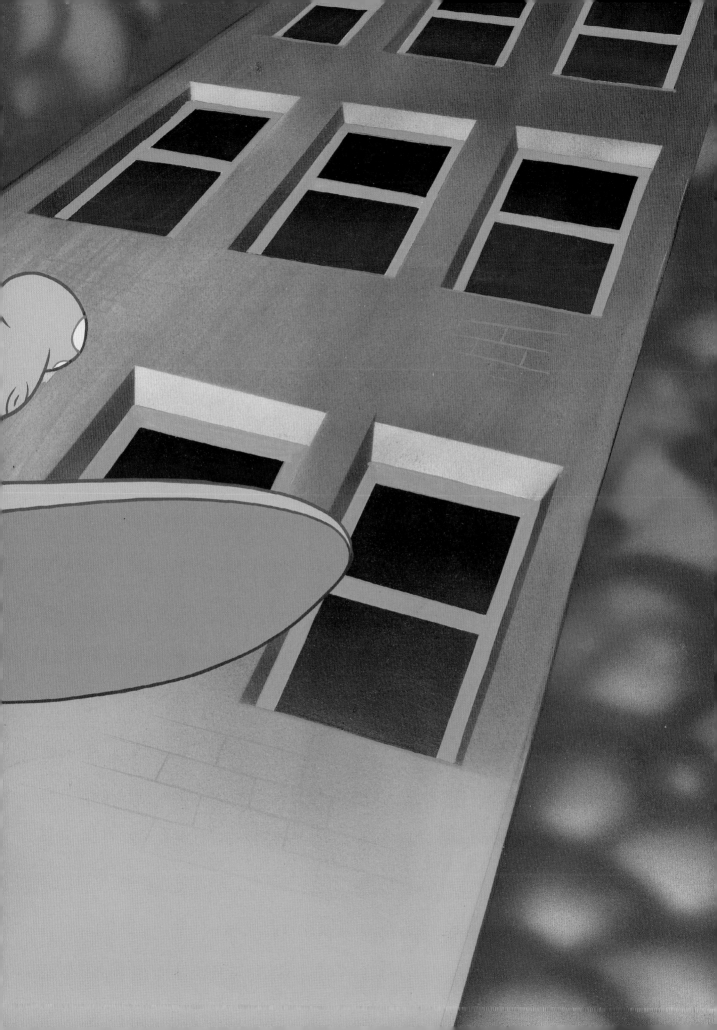

With the wind whistling
past as they sped toward the
ground, Timothy quickly
told Dumbo that the magic
feather wasn't real. He didn't
need it. All he had to do was
believe in himself.

Whoosh! Dumbo opened his ears just before they hit the ground. The clowns, the Ringmaster, and the audience watched him in amazement. Timothy shouted for joy as Dumbo flew up, down, and all around the Big Top. He was a flying elephant!

Then Dumbo began to play. The astonished audience went wild as Dumbo zoomed after the clowns, chasing them around the ring. The crowd roared as he dove at the Ringmaster. They applauded thunderously as Dumbo did loop-the-loops and rolls and spins in the air, then he scooped up a bunch of peanuts and hurled them at the elephants.

"You're making history!" Timothy declared.

In the days that followed, Dumbo became the most famous elephant in the world.

The circus was more popular than ever. People came from all over to see the little elephant fly.

Timothy, who was now
Dumbo's manager, became
famous, too.
The two best friends made
the news around the world!

The Ringmaster freed Dumbo's mother and gave her and Dumbo a fancy car at the end of the circus train. For Dumbo, there was nothing more wonderful than being with his mother again. When she hugged him tight, he was the happiest elephant in the world.

Even though Dumbo was now a star, he would always be Mrs. Jumbo's baby.